You can Face your Fears

Written by

Daniel Kenney

Illustrated by

Sumit Roy

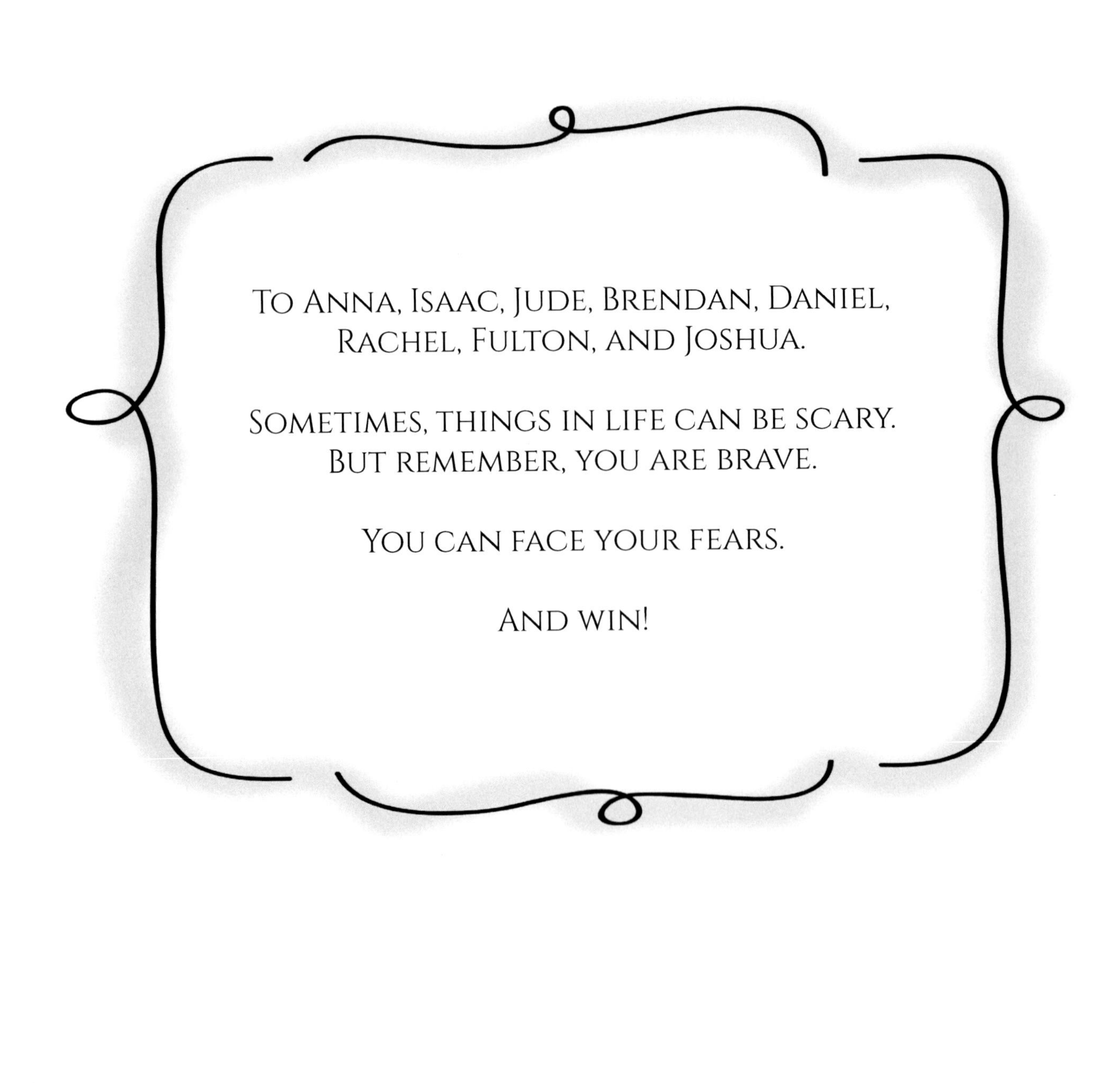

To Anna, Isaac, Jude, Brendan, Daniel, Rachel, Fulton, and Joshua.

Sometimes, things in life can be scary. But remember, you are brave.

You can face your fears.

And win!

THIS IS HENRY, AND SOMETIMES HE GETS SCARED.

Sometimes, Henry is scared of sleeping in a dark room.

THE SHADOWS REMIND HIM OF GHOSTS.

AND HE THINKS THERE ARE MONSTERS UNDER HIS BED.

But Henry needs to know something important.

HE IS BRAVE.

He can face his fears.

And win.

Sometimes, the toilet scares Henry.

It makes all sorts of weird noises.

AND HE'S WORRIED THE TOILET WATER WILL OVERFLOW.

But Henry needs to know something important.

HE IS BRAVE.

He can face his fears.

And win.

Sometimes, the dog next door scares Henry.

HE'S WORRIED THE DOG MIGHT JUMP UP
AND SLOBBER ALL OVER HIS FACE.

And maybe even bite.

But Henry needs to know something important.

HE IS BRAVE.

He can face his fears.

And win.

Sometimes, Henry is scared of going through the car wash.

He's worried it's really a giant squid monster.

THAT MIGHT ATTACK HIS CAR AND CARRY IT THROUGH THE CITY.

But Henry needs to know something important.

HE IS BRAVE.

He can face his fears.

AND WIN.

Sometimes, the dentist scares Henry.

He's worried the dentist will use his tools to turn him into Frankenstein.

OR THAT THE DENTIST DRILL WILL REALLY HURT.

But Henry needs to know something important.

HE IS BRAVE.

SO BRAVE!

He can face his fears.

AND WIN.

Sometimes, things in life can be scary.
But remember, you are brave.
You can face your fears.
And win!

Instructions For Parents and Trusted Adults:

Being inspired to face our fears is important. But what do we do next?

Step One: Admit our fears.

Everyone is afraid of something. Even adults. Think of a fear you have. Now consider sharing it with the child so they know adults have fears too, just like them.

Great. Now it's the child's turn. Help the child think of a fear he or she might have. Remember, the point isn't to scare the child. If they say they don't have a fear, that's great. But if they do have a fear, then admitting it can be the first step toward facing it.

Step Two: Exposure.

Gradually exposing yourself to your fear over time is how most of us get over our fears. For example, a child who is afraid of sleeping in the dark might overcome that fear by gradually, over time, being exposed to less and less light in his or her bedroom at night.

Share with your child how you overcame a fear—or how you intend to overcome a current fear. Then help the child think about how they might face their own fear. How could the child gradually face that fear over time?

Published by Trendwood Press
ISBN: 978-1-947865-15-0

Cover: Alchemy Book Covers
Illustrations: Sumit Roy
Interior formatting: Polgarus Studio

Made in the USA
Middletown, DE
20 October 2018